The Boxcar Children Mysteries

THE HONEYBEE MYSTERY

created by
GERTRUDE CHANDLER WARNER

Illustrated by Hodges Soileau

ALBERT WHITMAN & Company
Morton Grove, Illinois

Activities by Bonnie Bader
Activity illustrations by Alfred Giuliani

ISBN 0-8075-3374-2

1 3 5 7 9 10 8 6 4 2

Printed in the U.S.A.

Contents

CHAPTER 1

An Unpleasant Surprise

"I have to admit," Grandfather confessed as he drove along, "I've been thinking about it all week."

"We know you have," Jessie told him, watching the green farmland roll by her window. "We're almost as excited as you are."

"This is the best honey in the world," he said for about the hundredth time, looking at Benny and Violet in the little mirror. Henry was belted into the seat next to him. "The very best." Grandfather actually licked his lips. "Oh, I can't wait."

Visiting the small roadside stand at the front of Sherman Farm had become a yearly tradition for James Alden. He had noticed it coming home one evening and decided to check it out. It was only a few miles from his house.

Grandfather, who had always loved honey, decided to buy a jar of their home-made brand. He put it on toast that night and enjoyed it so much that he came back the next day and bought another jar. He made a promise never to miss the first harvest in early summer, when the season's honey was fresh.

He pulled alongside the stand and parked the car. All four doors opened, and James Alden and his four grandchildren filed out.

"Boy, it sure is hot today," Henry remarked. "Really hot." At fourteen, Henry was the oldest of the Alden children. He was a handsome dark-haired boy who kept a careful watch on his younger brother and sisters.

"It sure is," Jessie agreed. "When we get home, maybe we should mix a big pitcher of lemonade. It'll be good for all of you on a day like this." Jessie, at twelve, was the second oldest child. She was always thinking about everyone else.

"Lemonade, yum!" Benny exclaimed as they made their way toward the front of the white-painted stand. Six-year-old Benny was the youngest Alden, but he had the biggest appetite in the family. Benny loved good food — and in Benny's eyes, good food meant *any* food. "Lemonade and honey! What a day!"

Violet, the second youngest Alden at ten, reached the front of the stand before everyone else. She was a pretty girl with long dark hair and a calm, pleasant face. Her name suited her perfectly, for violet was her favorite color. But she was attracted to all things colorful. She loved to paint and draw and had a keen eye for beauty.

"Lemonade sounds like a great idea, Jessie," she said with a smile. "I think I'd like — oh, no!"

She stopped suddenly, and the rest of the Alden crew hurried up behind her. Then they saw what she saw, and their mouths dropped open.

The stand was shut tight, and at the front someone had thumbtacked a hastily made sign:

NO HONEY THIS YEAR
SORRY

"No honey . . . ?" Jessie said. "Oh, no."

All the children turned to their grandfather, who was staring at the sign.

"I can't believe it. No honey?"

Violet came up alongside him and patted him on the back. "Sorry, Grandfather."

"We can get some at the store," Henry suggested weakly.

"Supermarket honey?" Grandfather asked. "No, Henry, that wouldn't be the same."

"Maybe we can make some for you!" Benny suggested.

"Not unless we turn into bees we can't," Henry said.

"Bees? Bees make the honey?"

"Yes," Henry told him. "I'll explain it later."

"Okay."

Grandfather let out a long, weary sigh. "Oh, well, that's the way it goes, I guess. Everyone ready to go back home?"

"Sure," Jessie said sadly, wishing there was something they could do.

The Aldens started toward the car. Then Grandfather turned back to look at the sign one more time. "I wonder *why* there isn't any honey this year," he said quietly. "I wonder what happened."

Much to everyone's surprise, he got an answer. "I'll tell you what happened!" a stranger's voice replied. "My bees stopped doing their job!"

From around the other side of the stand, a man in overalls appeared. His white hair was a mess, and his face was red and shiny with perspiration.

He snapped his fingers. "Just like that," he told the Aldens, "nothing! They up and quit on me!"

Grandfather smiled and put his hand out.

"I'm James Alden. I take it you're Clay Sherman."

The man shook Grandfather's hand while using the other to pat his forehead with a folded handkerchief. "That's right. I am the unfortunate owner of this farm." He pointed in the direction of his fields. "And of those lazy bees."

"That's too bad," Grandfather said. "You must be very disappointed."

"You bet I am," Mr. Sherman replied.

"Our grandfather is disappointed, too," Benny piped up. "He loves your honey. He gets some fresh every year!"

"Oh, is that so?"

Grandfather nodded. "I do come here at least once a year around this time, yes."

"You like it that much?" Mr. Sherman asked.

"You have no idea," Jessie told him. "It's the only thing he's talked about all week."

The other children laughed. "He's honey happy!" Benny said with a grin.

James Alden smiled at his grandchildren's good-natured teasing. "I have to admit, Mr.

Sherman, I've never had honey as good as yours. I think it would be safe to say it's my favorite honey in the world."

Mr. Sherman nodded and smiled. "Well, what can I say to that? I certainly can't disappoint one of my most loyal customers, now, can I?"

"What do you mean?" Henry asked.

Mr. Sherman turned away, motioning for the Aldens to follow. "Come on inside the house. I've got something I think you'll like."

"Is it honey for Grandfather?" Benny asked excitedly.

Mr. Sherman looked back at the boy with a gleam in his eye.

"Maybe."

The Alden children lived happily with their grandfather in his home in Greenfield, Connecticut. But they hadn't always enjoyed such a happy life. Their parents died when they were younger, and they soon found themselves with nowhere to go. So they journeyed into some nearby woods, where they eventually came upon an abandoned boxcar. They made it their new home. It was very old, but they cleaned it and brightened it up with flowers. But they couldn't live there forever.

One day their grandfather came looking for them. But they didn't know him then, and they thought he didn't like them. So they hid, hoping he would eventually give up looking for them and leave.

But their grandfather was very determined, and once the children realized what a kind person he was, they happily agreed to live in Greenfield with him, along with their beloved dog, Watch. Grandfather even set up the boxcar in his backyard so they could play in it anytime they wished. It was a reminder of the hard life they once had, and the happy one they had now.

The kitchen in the Shermans' farmhouse was very similar to the Aldens' kitchen — large and airy, with lots of sunlight. Mr. Sherman invited the Aldens to sit around a wooden table in the center of the room. His wife, Dottie, joined them, too. She was a tall, silver-haired woman with bright eyes and a lively smile. The children liked her immediately. Jessie and Violet were particularly drawn to her. They would soon discover she did as much to help run the farm as her husband did.

"So, what exactly happened with the bees?" Jessie asked, using a straw to swirl a glass of lemonade Dottie had poured for her. The ice cubes jingled musically against the glass.

Clay Sherman threw his hands up in frustration. "I have absolutely no idea! Dottie and I have been doing this for going on thirty years now, and we've never seen anything like it!"

Grandfather took a bite from a piece of honey-coated toast. His gift from the Shermans for being such a faithful customer was, as Benny had guessed, a jar of last year's honey. It tasted just as good as ever.

"Do the bees seem to be acting any differently?" Grandfather asked.

Dottie shook her head. "No, not really."

"Everything had been going just fine,"

Clay said. "We did the same things we do every year. The wildflowers in the back field were growing normally; the weather has been okay. Sometimes bad weather can throw the bees off a bit, especially if there's a lot of rain. But there wasn't too much this year. In fact, I told Dottie that this looked to be one of the best honey seasons we've ever had."

Dottie nodded, remembering this.

"And then . . . ?" Henry asked.

"Then . . ." Clay put his hands up again. "Who knows? I can't explain what's been happening out there. The bees aren't making any honey. They're just making this whitish liquid instead. It looks a little like milk with water added to it. It's almost like . . . like honey that isn't getting sticky or thick."

"Have you talked to a bee expert?" Violet asked.

Clay nodded resignedly. "Yes, I've called a few people I know. Everyone's stumped. This seems to be a new problem. No one's ever heard of it before." The white-haired man rubbed the sides of his head, as if he had a bad headache.

"And the worst part," he said with a long, weary sigh, "is the business we're going to lose." He looked at the children sadly.

"You mean from the honey you sell around here?" Henry asked. "Is it that much?"

Clay Sherman actually laughed, but not in a funny way. His wife patted him on the back.

"No, Henry, not from buyers around here. As much as Dottie and I love customers like your family, we make most of our money from the honey we sell to the West Star Supermarket chain."

James Alden was surprised. "You mean the one that has stores all along the western coast of the country?"

Clay nodded. "That's the one. We sell most of our honey to them each year."

Grandfather went on, "They're one of the fastest-growing supermarket chains in America. If you do business with them now . . ."

Dottie already knew what James Alden was thinking. "We can do even more later on, when they get really big."

"But there's a good chance we'll *lose* their business if we don't give them our honey this year," Clay said.

"When do you have to do that?" Henry asked.

Clay looked up at the calendar hanging over the stove. "We have to have a definite answer for them in about two weeks."

"*Two weeks?*" Jessie blurted. "How are you going to do that?"

"That's the problem," Dottie answered. "It doesn't seem like we will."

"Why two weeks?" Grandfather asked.

"That's about when Mr. Price, the buyer for West Star, usually comes here," Clay told him. "John Price is a good man. He heard how delicious our honey was. Then, when he got the job of buying products for West Star, he remembered us. Now he comes around each year with a new contract, and he always makes good on his promises." Clay held a finger up. "Kids, remember, the only kind of people you should ever do business with are the ones who keep their promises."

Dottie continued, "Mr. Price said he'd keep giving us our yearly contract, no matter how much honey West Star needed, as long as we could keep making it. He's always kept up his end of the bargain."

Clay's shoulders sank. "And until now, we've always kept up ours. I just don't know what we're going to do. If we can't fix this problem, John will have to buy from someone else."

"Would he really do that, after all these years?" Jessie asked.

"He'd have no choice," Dottie told her.

Grandfather Alden shook his head. "That's too bad, Clay."

"Tell me something," Henry said. "If you could figure out what was wrong with those bees and fix it, would you still be able to make enough honey for Mr. Price this year?"

Clay thought about it for a moment. "Well, it'd be tight, but we could probably manage it, yes. I mean, we've lost a lot of time already, but then we always plan for more time than we really need."

He threw his hands up again. "But what does it matter? I don't know what to do! Neither Dottie nor I know any more about this problem than we did when it started a few weeks ago. If you've got something in mind, we're all ears."

Henry, leaning against the sink, tapped his chin thoughtfully. "You know, I think maybe I do. How about letting us take a look around to see what we can find? We're sort of detectives, you know."

Clay's eyebrows rose. "You are?"

Benny smiled. "Yep. We've solved lots of mysteries!"

"There hasn't been one yet they couldn't figure out," Grandfather added seriously.

Clay looked at his wife. She shrugged her shoulders and nodded.

"Well, why not?" he said, getting up from the table. "If you can solve this little mystery, you can have all the honey you want. How about that?"

"Grandfather would love that," Violet said.

"Okay, then," Clay said as he led them out the door and into the sunny afternoon. "Let me take you out back and show you what's going on."

CHAPTER 2

"Don't Sneeze, Henry!"

The Shermans kept their bees in a grove of oak trees behind one of the cornfields. On the other side of the grove was a gently sloping meadow filled with beautiful wildflowers.

"We never planned to go into the bee business," Clay told the Aldens, "but not long after we bought this farm, one of our neighbors came over and said, 'You know, the last owner always thought that field of wildflowers would be a perfect place to keep bees.' So Dottie and I decided to give it a try."

In and around the grove were about fifty artificial beehives. They looked like small, rectangular towers. Each tower was actually a stack of boxes, and each box contained a separate hive. Hundreds of little brown bees buzzed around them.

"What's this thing over here?" Benny asked, pointing to a low, square table upon which sat a large basket that was shaped kind of like an igloo.

"Oh, that's called a skep," Clay told them. "It's an old-style beehive. Apiarists — that's the fancy word for beekeepers — used to house their bees in those things a long time ago, before these modern hives were invented."

"Do the bees still use it?" Violet asked.

"I don't think so," Clay said. "I see them going in there sometimes, but once they build a hive in one of these boxes, that's where they stay. I just keep that one around as sort of an antique."

Jessie nodded. "That's neat."

"When you work with the bees, do you have to touch them?" Benny asked.

Dottie said, "We sure do. We have to move the hives around once in a while and remove the honeycomb frames to get the honey out."

"But you wear gloves, right?"

"No, gloves are too hard to work with. They get sticky and dirty, and you can't really feel anything with them on." She wiggled her fingers. "We need to be able to feel the bees in case they get caught under our hands."

"But don't they sting you?" Benny asked, alarmed.

Clay smiled. "Every now and then you get a sting, but that's rare. The main rule is to move slowly. Quick movements frighten the bees, and when they sting it's almost always because they're scared."

"Bees are much more peaceful and gentle than most people think," Dottie told the Aldens. "They don't want to sting anyone.

They only do that when they feel they have to. If you treat them with respect, they'll treat you with respect."

"I haven't been stung in ages," Clay added.

Then he said, "So, do you want to see how all this works?"

"We sure do," Jessie replied.

"Okay. . . ."

He put on the protective headgear that he'd brought along. It really wasn't much more than a hat with a net hanging down to protect his face and neck.

He looked at the Alden children and smiled. "Like something from outer space, huh?"

"Yeah, creepy!" Benny said.

"This is just for safety. Getting stung on the hand is one thing. Getting stung on the face is worse."

He went over to see one of the hives and gently removed the lid from the top box. The buzzing sound became a bit louder. As Clay set the lid against the side of the hive, hundreds of bees turned their attention to him. They crawled on his arms and legs and around the netting on his hat.

"The first time I did this, I was so scared I was shaking."

Jessie brushed some imaginary bees off her body. "Ooo, I don't think I'd like that feeling at all!"

"Oh, I don't know," Violet said. "There's something special about it, being so close to animals like that."

"I have to admit," Dottie said, particularly to Jessie, "I didn't like the idea at first, either. But I got used to it. As long as the bees aren't mad at you, you get the feeling they're kind of . . . well, affectionate."

"I wonder if they know who you are," Henry said.

Clay said, "I sometimes wonder that, too. If so, I'm sure they're plenty used to Dottie and me by now."

He reached into the hive box, even more slowly this time, and took out what looked like a picture frame. But instead of a picture, it held a honeycomb that was alive with hundreds of bees.

"This is called a comb," he said. "I keep ten of these in each hive, and each one contains about six thousand cells. Each cell has six sides."

"Do the bees live in those cells?" Benny asked.

"Yes and no," Dottie replied. "They live in the hive, and they certainly go into the cells a lot. But mostly they use the cells to store honey and wax, and the queen lays eggs that hatch into more worker bees."

"Worker bees?" Jessie said. "What are they?"

"Every hive has the queen, the drones, and the workers," Clay told her. "The queen lays the eggs and is the leader of the group. The drones do their part, too, but it's the workers that do most of the actual work, as you can guess by their name."

"What kind of work?" Violet asked.

"They fly out and collect nectar," Dottie told her. "They build the combs, make the honey and wax, feed the queen, and care for her eggs."

"Sounds like a lot," Benny said.

Dottie nodded. "It sure is."

Henry, who was thinking about the mystery at hand, asked, "So how exactly does the honey-making process work?"

Clay looked up and smiled. "See that other hat?" he asked, pointing toward the tree stump where it lay.

"Yeah."

"Put it on and I'll show you."

Henry's eyes widened. "Really?"

"Sure. You're the oldest. Think you can do it?"

"I guess so."

Clay added, "A real detective would want to know everything he could firsthand."

Henry nodded. "That's true. Okay." He walked over and carefully put on the net hat. His brother and sisters giggled at him.

"You look like a spaceman!" Benny teased.

"Very funny. What do I do now?"

"Come on over here," Clay said, "and I'll show you what happens."

Henry was a little nervous, but he trusted

Clay and moved slowly. Still, as that buzzing sound grew louder and louder, and the bees started landing on his bare arms . . .

"The first thing a bee does to make honey is fly out into that field of wildflowers. It lands on a flower and collects the flower's nectar. Then the worker bee flies back here. Now hold this comb up so everyone can see it."

Clay carefully handed the comb to Henry, who made a point of moving very slowly. He took care to make sure there were no bees under his fingers when he took the frame. The bees seemed less interested in Clay now and more interested in Henry. It wasn't long before they were crawling all over him.

"You doing okay?" Clay asked.

Henry smiled, but was careful not to move his body. "Yeah, sure. Doing great."

"Good, good."

Jessie shivered. "I don't know if I could keep so still!"

"I think it's neat," Violet said, her eyes sparkling with excitement.

"Don't sneeze, Henry!" Benny said. "And don't itch, either."

"Thanks, Benny," Henry said. "I'll try to remember that."

Benny turned and peered into the old-fashioned, igloo-shaped beehive behind them. "Is there any honey in here?"

Henry, Jessie, and Violet turned and looked more closely at the old straw skep.

"I doubt that, Benny," said Clay. Smiling, he continued, "Once a worker bee has a full honey stomach, it flies back to the hive and deposits the nectar into one of these cells." He pointed to one of the empty ones. It was about the size of the holes on the side of a piece of notebook paper.

"How does it get the nectar out of its honey stomach?" Benny asked.

"Well, if you must know . . . it sort of spits it out."

Jessie made a face and put a hand on her own stomach. "Lovely."

Clay shrugged. "What can I tell you? That's how they do it. Anyway, they put the nectar into one of these cells, and then they seal the cell with wax. Bees also make wax, by the way. I guess you figured that out on your own."

"We knew about beeswax," Jessie said. "We've heard people say, 'Mind your own beeswax.'"

"I say that to Clay all the time," Dottie said. Everyone laughed, even Henry.

"That's right, she does," Clay replied. "And that's when I come out here."

"Very funny, Clay," Dottie said.

"Thank you, dear."

"What happens to the nectar once it's in the cell?" Violet asked.

"While the nectar is in the bee's honey stomach, certain chemicals are added to it. Then, while the nectar is in the cell, the water in the nectar disappears and the chemicals from the bee's stomach blend with the nectar to create honey. It's actually pretty simple."

Henry said, "But obviously that's not happening here, right?"

Clay nodded. "That's right. For some reason the honey isn't forming." Clay reached under one of the hive boxes and pulled out a tray. It was filled with an off-white fluid that looked like watery milk.

"This is what I've been getting instead of honey. It's not getting thick." He poured it onto the ground and replaced the tray.

"What a mess!" Benny said.

"Sure is. This stuff keeps flooding the trays, and the bees aren't too happy, I'm sure. But I don't know *why* it's happening. *That's* the mystery.

"But anyway, now that you all understand the basics of beekeeping, what do you think? Any ideas?" He took the comb back from Henry and returned it to the hive box. Once all the bees had flown away, Henry removed his hat and gave a big sigh of relief.

"I think we should follow the order of how the bees make their honey to look for clues," Jessie announced.

"Sounds like a smart plan," Dottie said.

"I agree," Henry added. "If we sort of follow the bees through each step, we might come across something unusual."

"So where do we start?" Benny asked.

"In the field of flowers," Violet answered. "Right?"

"Right," Henry said with a single nod.

"While you're doing that," Clay said, "I've got to go take care of some things in the barn."

"And I've got to do some work in the house," Dottie added.

"Maybe I can lend a hand while my grandchildren do their clue hunting," Grandfather said. "What do you say, Clay? Could you use some help?"

"Sure," Clay answered, patting Grandfather on the back. "Come on."

CHAPTER 3

The First Clue

The field of wildflowers was much bigger than it first looked, as the Alden children quickly found out. They split up in order to cover more ground and agreed to meet back at the beehives in an hour.

By the time Violet, who was almost to the very end of the field, first checked her watch, the hour was nearly up. She hadn't found anything unusual and was already beginning to think maybe the first clue was waiting for them in the next step — after the bees brought the nectar back to the hive and put it in the honeycomb cells.

Even though she was officially looking for clues to a new mystery, she had to admit she was enjoying this walk through all these bright and colorful flowers, and on such a beautiful blue day, too! More than once she wished she'd brought along her sketch pad and pencils.

She reached the spot where the flowers ended and the pine forest began, took a quick look around, and saw nothing.

"Well, that's that," she said to herself. "I guess I should — "

No, wait, what's that over there?

She walked to the corner of the field and was surprised to find a small patch of wildflowers that were not very colorful at all — in fact, they were dried and shriveled, very much dead. What happened here? Was this a clue?

Anything unusual could be a clue, her detective's voice reminded her.

She knelt down, picked up one of the dead flowers, and rubbed it between her fingers. Then she gave it a sniff. Nothing unusual there, but then she wasn't a plant expert. She wasn't even sure what she should be looking for.

She checked her watch again and saw that the hour was up. So she gathered up a handful of the dead flowers and headed back.

"Hmm, I've never seen a dead patch in the meadow before," Clay said, stroking his chin. "How about you, Dot?"

"No, this is new to me." She was sitting at the kitchen table with one of the flowers laid out neatly on a sheet of white paper. Her glasses were down almost to the tip of her nose.

"Do you ever use any pesticides?" Henry asked. "Anything that might have this kind of effect on wildflowers?"

"What are pesticides?" Benny asked.

"They're chemicals used to kill bugs that eat the crops," Jessie told him. "Some bugs will destroy entire fields of fruits and vegetables if they're not sprayed with pesticides, isn't that right?"

"Exactly right," Dottie told her.

"Oh, I get it," Benny said.

Clay shook his head. "But we don't use them much anymore," he said. "Sometimes in the spring if the bugs are really bad, but not now. And certainly not on the wildflowers."

"That would have a bad effect on the nectar, right?" Violet asked.

"Not just that," Dottie told her. "The bees would probably die."

"That wouldn't be very nice," Benny decided.

"No, it wouldn't," Dottie agreed.

"What about accidentally?" Violet suggested. "Maybe the wind carried some of the chemicals down to the flowers while you were spraying one day."

Clay shrugged his shoulders. "I suppose it's possible."

Henry shook his head. "But not in this case, because why would only that one spot be affected? Why not the whole field? And like Mrs. Sherman said, the bees would have died."

Dottie nodded. "Henry's right, Clay. If pesticides did this, most of our bees would have died."

"So that rules out pesticides," Jessie said. She rubbed some of the dead leaves between her fingers. It left a chalky yellow coloring. "Violet, did you notice this?"

"What?"

"This yellow stuff."

Violet looked closely at her sister's fingers. "No, I didn't. That's unusual. I did the same thing, and that didn't happen to me."

"It's not on all of them," Jessie said. "Just some."

Clay took one of the yellowed flowers and gave it a sniff. "Ooo, that smells awful!"

"Is it anything familiar?" Henry asked.

"No," said Clay, "I don't think so."

Grandfather, who had been standing by the back door, snapped his fingers. "I've got an idea! There's a chemical lab in town. The daughter of a friend of mine works there, a nice young woman named Renee Trowbridge. She might be able to tell us what that stuff is."

"Do you think she'd mind?" Clay said.

"No, not at all."

"Well, if she can help us, I'll give her some honey, too."

"Oh, boy, a real laboratory!" Benny said with a big smile. "Cool!"

"It's really very interesting," his grandfather told him. "Would you care to come along?" he asked the Shermans.

"We certainly would," Dottie replied. "The sooner we can get to the bottom of this, the better."

"Okay, let's go."

Benny had seen a chemical laboratory only once, and that was in a spooky movie that he and Henry watched one night. There were lots of bubbling, smoking liquids in glass tubes, and lightning bolts kept flashing outside. The mad scientist who worked there was scary, with wild hair and an evil chuckle.

But there were no mad scientists working at ChemCo, which was the name of the lab in town. Instead there was a young woman with blond hair and a warm smile. This was Renee, Grandfather's friend. She wore a long white lab coat and had a pair of goggles hanging from a strap around her neck. Much to Benny's relief, she didn't have an evil laugh.

"You say you found these in a field of flowers that were otherwise healthy?" she asked.

Violet nodded. "That's right. There was a patch about this wide." She spread her arms as far as they would go. "All the flowers in there were dead. They were lying on the ground, all yellowed and curled. But all the other flowers around this spot were fine."

"Hmmm." Renee got up onto a tall stool behind one of the heavy lab tables. There was a microscope on it. Much to Benny's delight, there also were rows of glass tubes containing colorful chemical liquids. None of them smoked or bubbled, though.

"That's very strange, I have to admit," Renee said.

She tore off a small piece of the dead flower and trapped it between two glass slides. Each slide was about the size and shape of a stick of gum. Then she slipped it under the microscope and twisted a little knob to focus it.

"Okay, let's see now . . . I see the yellow stuff you mentioned. It doesn't look like something the flower would make, so it must have come from somewhere else."

She got up and went to a steel cabinet, from which she took three small plastic bottles. Each contained a different colored liquid. Then she returned to the table and tore off another piece of the dead flower.

"What's that you're doing?" Jessie asked.

"A few little tests," Renee said. "Maybe I can determine what that yellow stuff is."

She held the first bottle over the sample and squeezed out a single drop of clear fluid. Then she put the slide back into the microscope.

"Anything?" Clay asked.

"Mmm . . . no, not really. No reaction at all." She looked up and smiled.

She did the same thing using the next bottle, which had a pink fluid. "Hmmm, that's interesting," she mumbled to herself.

"What? What's interesting?" Jessie asked.

"Hang on. One more test. . . ."

The liquid in the last bottle was a sky-blue color. *Very pretty*, Violet thought, wondering what it was.

Renee's smile faded when she looked into the microscope this time. The others noticed this and fell silent.

"Oh, my goodness. These flowers have been sprayed with Menadrin!"

Jessie's face crumpled with confusion. "Menadrin? What's that?"

"It's an experimental chemical created a few years ago. It was supposed to make farm crops grow more quickly and produce larger fruits and vegetables, but government tests showed that it was unsafe, so they wouldn't allow it to be sold anywhere."

"Would it have any effect on bees?" Henry asked.

"Bees? I'm not sure."

"How about on the way they make honey?"

Renee thought for a moment, then nodded. "Yes, I think it would. Honey would go from being like glue to — "

"Being more like water?" Jessie suggested.

"Yes, something like that."

Grandfather snapped his fingers. "Now we're getting somewhere!"

"We sure are," Clay said, although he didn't appear quite as enthusiastic.

Renee looked back into the microscope. "I'll run some more tests just to be sure, but I'm positive this is Menadrin. And I have to admit I'm very surprised. I haven't heard anything about this stuff in years. I thought it was long gone."

"I guess the bees got it into their system by landing on these flowers," Henry suggested.

Renee nodded. "That makes sense. It must have mixed with the nectar they were collecting. Because it has this strange odor, it probably attracts bees. They probably love it. And the worst part is, the effect can be passed along."

"What do you mean?" Benny asked.

"I mean if one bee is infected by it and returns to the hive, all the bees will become infected."

"There's another part to this we haven't thought about," Henry said gravely.

All eyes turned to him. "What's that, Henry?" Grandfather asked.

"How the Menadrin got on the flowers in the first place." Henry paused to look at everyone, hoping they would see what he was driving at. "It had to have been put there by someone on purpose."

Violet's hands went to her mouth. "Oh, no!"

Henry nodded. "Oh, yes."

"One thing I know for sure about Menadrin," Renee said, "is that it was made in very small quantities, and it's almost impossible to find now. So, yes, the only way it could have gotten onto these flowers is if someone put it there on purpose."

"Just like that?" asked Clay.

Renee nodded. "Just like that."

Clay ran his fingers through his hair. "Oh, boy," he said, and sighed again.

CHAPTER 4

A Giant Suspect

The mood in the Aldens' station wagon was quiet on the way back to the farm. Grandfather turned on the radio but kept it low.

"Mr. Sherman, it seems pretty certain that someone sprayed a section of your wildflowers with Menadrin," Henry said.

"Yes, it does."

"Do you have any idea who it might have been?"

"No, can't say I do. Seems like a mighty mean thing for a person to do."

"No kidding," Violet said. "Those poor bees."

"And poor us," Clay said. "We're going to lose a lot of money this year."

Henry stroked his chin. "*Why* would someone do it?"

"Because they're mean," Clay said firmly, as if that explained everything.

"With any crime, there has to be a reason," Henry explained.

"Most of the time," Jessie continued, "someone has something to gain by what they're doing."

"Exactly," Henry said, nodding to his sister. "So who would have the most to gain by your bees producing no honey this year?"

Clay put his hands out. "I don't know."

"If you lost your contract with Mr. Price," Henry went on, hoping to lead the Shermans in the right direction, "who would get it?"

Clay looked at Dottie, but she didn't seem to have any answers, either.

"I have no idea. The only other person around here who keeps bees for honey is — hey, wait just a minute!"

Clay's eyes widened in surprise first, then they narrowed and darkened. "Jack Hennessey," he said flatly. "That's who would benefit. Of course!" He looked at Dottie again. "Why didn't we think of him before?"

"Jack Hennessey?" Grandfather asked, looking at the Shermans in the rearview mirror. "Who's that?"

"Clay — " Dottie started saying, but he didn't seem to hear.

"Jack Hennessey is a dirty, no-good scoundrel. He's got the farm next to ours. If you walk through that pine forest you saw at the end of the flower field, eventually you'll come to a road that leads to the back of *his* farm."

"Clay — " Dottie tried again.

"Jack Hennessey and I used to be partners in the farming business. We had our two farms, a nice colony of bees, everything. And we made good money, too. And then . . ." Clay's voice trailed off. Everyone waited for the rest, but it didn't come.

"And then . . . ?" Grandfather prompted. "And then what, Clay?"

Clay Sherman seemed restless now, nervous. "And then . . . well, we weren't partners anymore, and let's just leave it at that."

"Does he know about your honey contract with Mr. Price?" Jessie asked.

"Oh, you bet he does," Clay replied quickly. "He knows what it's worth, and you can believe he wants it. Yes, sir, he sure would benefit very much from my bees producing no honey this year. That . . . that . . ."

"Clay," Dottie said again, "we don't need to go into all the details about how you feel about Jack Hennessey. That was a long time ago, and to be fair, you have to admit that you're still not sure about everything that happened."

Clay folded his arms and said, "Well . . . maybe that's true, but that doesn't mean he wouldn't do something like this to me."

"He does seem like a possible suspect, Mrs. Sherman," Henry said.

"We can't ignore the possibility," Jessie added. "We have to check it out."

"I guess so," Mrs. Sherman agreed reluctantly.

"Tell you what," Grandfather said cheerfully. "I'll lend you my grandchildren for a few days, and they can take a real stab at this mystery. How about that?"

"Sounds good," Dottie agreed. "Clay?"

"Sure. I have no problems with it."

"Fine. I have to take care of some business matters of my own tomorrow, but maybe they can ride over to the farm on their bicycles first thing in the morning to see what they can find out. How does that sound?"

"Great," Clay said. "It's been a long time since we had youngsters on the farm. Our own kids have all grown up and moved away."

"If you come early enough, I'll make you

a real farmer's breakfast," Dottie told the Alden children. "Fresh eggs, fresh milk, the works."

"Ooo, now *that* I like!" Benny said.

"I figured you would," Violet cut in. "His stomach usually thinks before his head does," she told the Shermans, who managed to work up a little laughter in spite of themselves.

The children rode their bikes to the Shermans' farm early the next day, and Dottie, as promised, had a beautiful country breakfast waiting for them. There were piles of fried eggs, crisp bacon, steaming pancakes, plump biscuits, a tall pitcher of juice, and a bowl of delicious homemade maple syrup. She had it laid out on the big table in the kitchen over a red-and-white-checkered tablecloth. All the Aldens thanked Dottie for her kindness.

Jessie finished first and decided to take a walk around the farm to see some of the animals and see if she could find any clues. Maybe farm animals weren't as unusual as

the ones you'd see in a zoo, but at least you could pet them and get to know them over time. Jessie thought they'd become like members of the family after a while.

She visited the barn first and found two beautiful horses standing quietly in their roomy stalls. One was a shiny reddish-brown color, the other sleek black from head to toe. She petted their long noses and the black one licked her fingers.

Out behind the barn was the cow pasture. Clay had already done the milking for the day, and the wooden stool leaned against one of the posts. A steel bucket hung on a wood peg above it. Most of the cows were lying on the ground, with their legs tucked underneath, dozing peacefully in the morning sun. *No mystery here*, thought Jessie.

Jessie's next stop was a fenced-in area full of chickens and geese. The geese stayed in their own little group by a tiny pond in back, while the chickens clucked and strutted near the henhouse, pecking at the ground for food. Jessie went right up to the wire fence to watch them, and even the ones by her feet carried on with their business. *If something strange is going on at Sherman Farm*, Jessie thought, *it certainly isn't bothering the chickens.*

She was about to head back to the house when a movement in the cornfield caught her eye. When she looked again, she saw nothing. Maybe her eyes were playing tricks on her.

Then she saw movement again, and a moment later a large figure appeared. It was a man with dark hair wearing overalls and a straw hat that was way too small for his head. He was much bigger than Clay or Grandfather, or pretty much any other adult she'd ever seen.

But it wasn't his height that she found unusual — it was the way he was acting. He was looking all around, as if he were being hunted. He seemed very worried about being seen. And, Jessie noticed, he was heading in the direction of the bees.

When he reached the bee colony, he took something out of his pocket. But he was too far away for Jessie to tell what it was.

Now he seemed more nervous than ever. He stopped and looked around one last time. Then . . .

He's going into the wildflowers, she thought in astonishment. *I can't believe it.*

She waited until he was completely out of sight, then hurried back to the house to tell the others.

The Shermans and the Aldens watched out the kitchen windows as the large man returned from the field of wildflowers. He was still acting suspiciously, looking all around to make sure no one saw him. He went into the barn and returned with a silver pail. He took it to the chickens and began throwing feed to them.

Clay leaned back and stroked his chin. "Hmmm . . ."

"Who is he?" Violet asked.

"His name is George Cooper, but he prefers to be called Georgie. He's our hired hand. He came to us about a month ago. Answered an ad I put in the local paper for a laborer."

Henry looked interest. "A *month* ago?"

"Right around the time your bees stopped producing honey," Jessie said.

"Exactly," Henry said.

Clay and Dottie both nodded. "I've thought about that," Clay said, "but if Georgie was the one doing it, why would he still be here? Why would he hang around? When someone robs a bank, they don't sit out on the curb waiting for the police to show up."

"Maybe he's not done," Jessie suggested. The idea had a creepy feeling to it. "Maybe he's got other things planned, too."

"Would he have anything to gain, Mr. Sherman?" Violet asked. "Would he benefit by you losing the honey contract?"

Clay said, "To tell you the truth, I honestly couldn't say. I don't really know all that much about him."

The Aldens couldn't help noticing that Clay gave Dottie a very sheepish look. Dottie looked annoyed.

"He didn't have any references," she told the children.

"What are 'references'?" Benny asked.

Jessie explained, "References are people who can say what a good job you do. If you're trying to get a job, the people who might hire you will want some information about what kind of a person you are, so they talk to your references."

"Oh, I get it," said Benny.

Clay said, "He seemed nice enough to me, and he sure knew his way around a farm. He might not be very talkative, but he's a great worker. Strong as a bull. From watching him that first day, I could tell he'd done farm work before."

"Where does he live?" Henry asked.

"I believe he rents a room in town." He looked at Dottie again. "It's over the butcher shop, isn't it?"

Dottie shrugged. "I think so. It's hard to tell much about him. Like Clay said, he doesn't talk a lot. He keeps to himself. Only talks if you talk to him first. That makes me kind of nervous."

"Well, we're going down to the meadow to look for more clues," Henry said. "And we'll try to figure out what he was doing down there. If it looks like any of the flowers have been sprayed with anything, we'll let you know right away."

Dottie seemed happy with this. "And are you going to talk to him?" she asked her husband.

Clay shook his head. "No."

Dottie folded her arms. "And why not?"

"Because if he is the guilty one, I don't want him thinking we're suspicious of him. We've got to catch him red-handed. If he thinks we're on to him, he could disappear like that." Clay snapped his fingers.

Henry nodded. "He's right, Mrs. Sherman. For now we've got to act like we don't suspect a thing."

"But in the meantime, we'll keep a close eye on him," Jessie said.

CHAPTER 5

Spying Eyes

The Aldens spent the next few hours searching for more clues, but they had no luck.

They went into the wildflowers first, hoping to figure out what Georgie Cooper had been doing back there, but they found nothing. Georgie watched them from a distance, looking worried.

Toward the end of the afternoon, as Jessie and Henry were walking back to the Shermans' house, a car pulled up to the roadside stand. It was very large and expensive-looking. The man who got out was small and roundish, and he wore a tan suit. That was about all Henry and Jessie could see from where they were. The man went up to the stand, just as Grandfather had, and read the sign posted on the front. When he was finished, he started walking down the gravel driveway toward the house.

As Henry and Jessie went up to meet him, some of his other features became clear — he was older, with a full face and steel-rimmed glasses. He had removed his suit jacket and hung it over his arm. In his left hand was a folded handkerchief, which he was using to pat his neck and forehead.

When he reached the Aldens, he smiled and said, "Hello, there. I'm Bob Carlson." He sounded out of breath.

"Hi," Henry said, smiling back. "I'm Henry Alden, and this is my sister Jessie."

Mr. Carlson nodded. "Pleased to meet you both. Do you youngsters work on this farm?" He seemed very friendly, with his warm smile and easy voice.

"No, we're just visiting," Henry told him.

In spite of the man's friendliness, Henry thought it best to remain careful about what to say. There was no reason to tell a total stranger that he and his family were working on a mystery.

"Oh, I see. Well, would you happen to know what's going on with the honey? Why is it unavailable this year?"

"Do you come for it often?" Jessie asked.

He shook his head. "No, only about every six months. I have relatives not far from here, and each time I pass through, I stop by and get a jar or two."

"Just like our grandfather," Jessie said.

"Is that right? I'm not surprised. This honey is very good."

Henry said, "From what we've heard, the Shermans are having trouble with their bees."

The visitor looked puzzled. "Trouble? What kind of trouble?"

"I'm not sure. They just stopped making honey a few weeks ago. That's what we were told."

The man put his hands on his hips and

looked toward the beekeeping area. "That's a shame, it really is. They've got the best honey in the world, too. Such a shame."

Jessie nodded. "It sure is."

Mr. Carlson let out a long sigh. "Oh, well, maybe next time." He removed his hat and ran his arm across his brow. "Thanks anyway. It was nice meeting you."

"You too," Henry told him.

Just before Mr. Carlson turned away, he looked up at the sun and said, "Boy, it sure is hot today, isn't it?" He patted his neck with the handkerchief, then unbuttoned his cuffs and began rolling his sleeves up. As he did so, Henry and Jessie saw that his arms were covered with a nasty red rash.

They looked at each other but said nothing.

Henry and Jessie rounded up Violet and Benny and went back into the house to tell the Shermans about Mr. Carlson. Mr. Sherman sighed and said he felt bad to lose customers like that. "By this time next year," he said, "most of those customers will be buying their honey somewhere else."

The Aldens didn't have too much cheer to add to the conversation. They reported finding no more clues during their hot, day-long search. They stood by their bicycles in back of the house as the sun settled into the horizon behind them.

"We're sorry we didn't find more clues today," Jessie said, restlessly twisting the grips of her handlebars.

"Yeah, we looked *everywhere*," Benny assured them.

Dottie, standing with Clay on the back porch, smiled and nodded. "We know you did, and we're very grateful."

"Maybe we'll have better luck tomorrow," Violet suggested.

"Maybe," Clay said, trying to smile but finding it hard.

"Catching George Cooper sneaking around in the meadow was very good," Dottie said, trying to remain upbeat. "He just might be the one."

"I guess," Jessie said. "Then again, maybe he won't be."

"Well, let's go," Henry said. "It's going to

be dark soon, and Grandfather will want to know what — "

"Hey, look!" Benny said sharply, pointing toward the wildflowers.

A man was standing there, crouched low and obviously spying. And it wasn't Georgie, either. In fact, it wasn't anyone they recognized.

When he realized he'd been noticed, he froze, his eyes wide.

"Hey!" Henry shouted, and the man took off running.

"Oh, my goodness!" Dottie said.

"C'mon!" Henry commanded, breaking into a sprint.

The man fell forward and disappeared for a moment. The flowers above him were waving around crazily. Then he popped back up and kept going.

"Does he look familiar to you?" Jessie asked as she caught up to her brother.

"I didn't get a good look at him," Henry said breathlessly.

The Aldens reached the beekeeping area just as the man reached the end of the field and crossed into the pine forest. The children had to weave around the little hive towers as if they were running an obstacle course.

"What are we going to do if we catch up to him?" Jessie asked.

"Nothing," Henry told her. "I just want to get close enough to get a better look at him."

The Aldens entered the flower meadow and struggled through.

"He's getting away!" Violet cried.

"He won't get away," Henry said. He wasn't sure if this was true, but he didn't want his brother and sisters getting discouraged. "We'll catch up as soon as we get to the forest."

Unfortunately, the man had disappeared.

The Aldens came to a halt, scanning the area in every direction.

"Oh, no!" Violet cried. "We lost — "

"Shhh," Henry said quietly, holding his hand up. He smiled at Violet and said in almost a whisper, "Don't give up that easily. Listen."

The four of them stood with their knees bent slightly, ready to take off at any moment. Only their eyes moved.

"Where did he go?" Henry asked, still whispering.

Violet pointed to the right. "Over there."

Henry began stepping quietly in that direction. The pine needles crunched softly under his sneakers. "C'mon," he said softly.

They crept in a line, oldest to youngest, tallest to smallest. Benny took up the rear, searching in every direction with eyes wide open.

About fifty feet ahead of them there came a *whoosh* sound, like the swipe of a rake through a big pile of autumn leaves. Henry put his hand up to call for silence.

Another *whoosh*, and then the man leaped out from behind a tree and took off like a rabbit.

"There he is!" Benny cried.

At the front of the line now, Jessie led them through a maze of trees, shrubs, and large stones. Still no one had gotten a good look at the man.

At last they began to close the gap. From behind they could see that he was wearing faded blue jeans and a black-and-white-checkered shirt with the sleeves rolled up. He wore a black hat and had dark hair.

The man tripped over something and crashed to the forest floor. The Aldens were still a good distance away, but the man glanced back long enough for Henry to get a good look at his face. He had a thick mustache that ran all the way down to his chin and deep lines in his face. The man scrambled to his feet and kept going. The Aldens, now out of breath, slowed to a halt.

"Okay, I saw him," Henry said.

"I think we all did," Jessie told him.

"So now what do we do?" Violet asked.

"We go back and tell the Shermans. Maybe they know him."

"He's *got* to have something to do with it," Jessie said.

Henry nodded. "Yeah, most likely."

"Hey, do you hear that?" Benny asked. They all fell silent, and then an engine started up in the distance.

"A truck?" Jessie wondered.

"It must be on that road Mr. Sherman mentioned."

The vehicle shifted into gear, and then the sound of its engine faded into nothing.

"Okay, let's get back," Henry said. "And this time we walk. No running, okay?"

He received no argument from the others.

CHAPTER 6

Mascots

At dinner that evening, the children told Grandfather about the chase in the woods. They had returned home exhausted and were glad that Grandfather had ordered take-out chicken. "No reason why you should have to chase down supper tonight," he joked.

"You should have been in the woods with us, Watch," said Benny as he peered under the table at their dog. "You could've caught that man for sure."

"We didn't need to *catch* him," reminded

Henry. "We just needed to see who was sneaking around the farm and describe him to the Shermans."

"But Mr. and Mrs. Sherman said he didn't sound familiar at all," said Jessie glumly.

"And we don't know what to do next," sighed Violet.

"Any news from Renee at the lab?" Henry asked Grandfather.

"No, not yet." Grandfather shook his head. "It's certainly not a good sign. I'm afraid it's beginning to look as if we won't find a cure for what the Menadrin has done to the bees."

Jessie looked down at her plate. "I know. I just wish we knew who sprayed it on Clay Sherman's wildflowers in the first place."

"And *why*," added Henry.

They went to bed early that night and returned to the Shermans' farm early the next morning. Dottie had a breakfast feast waiting for them. And, like the day before, Jessie went out to see the animals after she'd finished eating.

As she stood by the fence that outlined the cow field, she was surprised to see Georgie Cooper, once again sneaking into the flowers.

"You must be kidding," she whispered to herself, crouching down. *He must know we're on to him*, she thought. *How could he be so careless?*

She wanted to run back to the house and tell the others what was happening. But then she thought, *No, this time I'm going to follow him by myself and see what he's up to. It'll be easier for one person to trail him than four.*

Once he was out of sight, Jessie followed the cow fence until she came to the opposite side of the field. She could just see the top of Georgie Cooper's head as he moved toward the end of it. Quietly she bent low and began pushing her way through the flowers.

She reached the end and stopped. Georgie was standing in a little clearing that someone had used as a dumping ground for old farm machinery. Everything

was heavily rusted and covered with twin-
ing vines and weeds. Jessie remembered
searching around it the day before with Violet, but they hadn't seen anything unusual.
From where she stood, Jessie had a perfect
view of Georgie — she could see him
clearly, but he wasn't able to see her.

He walked over to an old overturned
steel watering trough, bent down, and lifted
it about a foot off the ground with one
hand. Jessie was amazed — that trough
must have weighed about three hundred
pounds. That was more than the combined
weight of her, Henry, Violet, and Benny,
even *after* Benny ate dinner, she thought
with a grin.

Georgie looked around carefully, then
reached into the pocket of his overalls and
took something out. Again Jessie couldn't
see it.

Whatever it was, he slipped it under the
trough before setting it back down again.

He's trying to be quiet so no one will know,
Jessie thought. *Whatever he put under there,
he doesn't want anyone to know about it.*

There was a small hole at the rim of the trough right where Georgie had put whatever it was he'd had in his pocket. *It would be perfect for bees*, Jessie thought. What had Renee said? Menadrin attracts bees? This was a perfect way to get them to go after it — hide an open bottle of it under something heavy, something that looks like it hasn't been moved in a hundred years. Who would ever think of looking there? Maybe Georgie decided to do this after he realized they had found the dried Menadrin on the dead flowers.

Georgie looked around one last time, then headed back to the farmyard. Jessie waited a few minutes to make sure he was gone. Then she poked her head out of the sea of flowers. When she was sure he was out of sight, she crept back to the house.

"I'll fire him today!" Clay howled when Jessie explained what she'd seen. His face was as red as a boiled ham. "That double-crossing — "

"Clay," Dottie said calmly, "we're not even sure what he put under there."

The Aldens nodded. "That's right, Mr. Sherman," Jessie agreed. "I said it would be the perfect place to put more Menadrin, but I couldn't see anything clearly."

"What else could it be?" Clay barked, peering out the window over the kitchen sink, watching Georgie in the farmyard as he polished a leather saddle. "Why else would he be back there?"

"We should go find out, just to be sure," Henry said.

"But let's wait until Georgie goes to lunch," Dottie suggested. "That way he won't see us and get nervous."

Clay looked at his wife in surprise. "Why are you worried about him being nervous? You're the one who doesn't like him."

"I just don't want to do anything before we have the facts, that's all. The man should still be treated fairly."

Clay turned back to the window and frowned. "I guess," he grumbled.

So they waited, and as soon as Georgie

Cooper went to town on his lunch break, the Aldens and the Shermans ambled through the flowers to the farm-equipment graveyard.

"He lifted *this* with one hand?" Clay said, looking down at the old overturned trough.

Jessie nodded. "Uh-huh. Lifted it as if it were made of cardboard."

"How can one man do that?"

Henry got a hand under it and said, "Okay, I'm going to need some help here."

The Aldens lined up next to one another and wiggled their fingers underneath. When they were ready, Henry said, "Okay, here we go. One . . . two . . . *three!*"

They moaned and groaned and pulled their hardest, and slowly the trough began rising. Once it was high enough, Clay and Dottie wedged wooden poles under it to keep it up.

Wiping his hands off, Henry said, "Whew, that was pretty heav — "

"Oh, my goodness, look!" Violet said, pointing underneath.

There was no bottle of Menadrin any-

where in sight, nor any other kind of chemical that could stop bees from making honey. Instead there was one large gray-and-white cat with a family of tiny kittens attached to her belly, drinking her milk. The mother cat's eyes were wide with fear.

Benny smiled brightly. "Look at the kitties!" he cried delightedly.

"Oh, they're beautiful!" Violet declared.

"Food," Jessie said flatly, hands on her hips. "That had to be what he had in his pocket both times. He's been feeding them."

"And giving them milk," Dottie added. "Look at the bowl."

There was a small plastic bowl nearby filled with milk.

Clay took off his farmer's hat and scratched the top of his head. "Well, I'll be darned. Kittens. He was sneaking down here to feed them!" He looked at his wife. "I wonder why he hid them."

"He seems to have thought he'd get in trouble if we knew about them," Dottie said. "First I didn't like him, and then you didn't like him. He probably didn't want to take a chance that we'd be mad about the kittens."

Clay looked back at the furry family and shook his head. "We've had him figured all wrong, Dot. Both of us."

Dottie nodded reluctantly. "Yeah, we sure have."

CHAPTER 7

More Spying Eyes

When Georgie came back from lunch, the Aldens and the Shermans met with him in the farmyard and told him they found the mother cat and her kittens. For a moment he looked worried.

"Aw, gee, I'm sorry, Mr. Sherman. . . ." he said, in a voice that was surprisingly soft for a man of his size. "I was going to try and find a home for them myself, but the mama wouldn't budge, so I had to feed her, and check on her, and get her milk . . . and then I was worried you'd think I wasn't doing the job you hired me to do."

"Oh, Georgie, we're not mad at all," said Dottie, and the children could see that she and Clay felt bad about doubting Georgie. "In fact," she said, smiling at the kittens, "we're happy to have these new residents at Sherman Farm."

"I know a spot in the barn where we can set up a crate for them," said Clay. He showed Georgie a warm corner near the horse stalls, and before long they had carefully moved the cat family to their new home.

It would be part of Georgie's daily chores to make sure they had plenty of milk, food, and clean hay to sleep on. The Aldens thought they'd never seen anyone as happy as Georgie was when he heard all this.

In the Shermans' kitchen afterward, however, the good mood quickly drifted away.

"Okay, so if it wasn't Georgie, then it *has* to be Hennessey," Clay said, arms folded, leaning against the sink.

"How can you be so sure, Clay?" Dottie demanded.

"Because he's the only one left with a motive." He turned to the children. "Back me up on this. It *has* to be Hennessey, doesn't it?"

"Well . . ." Jessie began. She looked at Dottie. "He really does have the best motive."

Henry nodded. "Yeah, he's at the top of the suspect list."

"I'll bet that guy we chased through the woods the other day works for Mr. Hennessey," Benny suggested.

Clay snapped his fingers. "Hey, that's right! He did go back toward Hennessey's farm. I'll bet he does!"

"What we should do," Jessie said, "is the same thing he did — we should take a peek at their farm."

"If that guy was working for Mr. Hennessey, I wonder what he was doing here," Violet said.

"Probably spraying some more Menadrin," Clay replied.

Jessie shook her head. "I don't think so. I looked around when I was coming back from watching Georgie. I didn't see anything."

"I think he was just spying," Benny offered. "That's what it looked like he was doing."

Henry nodded. "That's what I thought, too."

"Then we should do a little spying of our own," Jessie said firmly.

Dottie sighed. "Well, I guess it won't hurt. Better to have some real evidence that it's them than to let you go over there yelling your head off," she said to Clay.

Clay smiled and put a hand lightly onto his chest. "Me? Yell my head off?"

"Oh, I forgot," Dottie replied, rolling her eyes. "You're such a cool-headed person."

The Aldens were enjoying this peculiar form of affection between the Shermans.

"Let's go check it out," Henry said, sliding out of his seat. The others got up and followed him out the door.

"Good luck," Clay said.

"And be careful," Dottie called through the window screen as they crossed into the farmyard. A chicken zoomed through their marching line, right between Jessie and Violet, clucking madly.

"We will," Jessie assured her.

The Aldens found the old back road to Hennessey's farm with no problem; it was just a little farther on from where they'd stopped chasing the spy the day before. It cut between the trees and was covered with gravel, coming to an end where the trees were too thick to cut through any farther. A little mound of dirt stood at the end of it.

Shortly the forest began to thin out on the right side, and they eventually came upon the Hennessey farm. It was just like the Shermans' in many ways — a large main house, a barn, and some fenced-in animal pastures.

The Aldens crept out of the sparse forest to get a closer look. The first thing they saw was another collection of ancient farm equipment. More rusty plows, water basins, and broken-down trucks.

"I guess all farms have a place like this," Benny said.

"Seems that way," Henry agreed.

They walked over to an old shed. The windows were either broken or missing completely, and there was no door. They peered inside and saw that the wooden floor was rotted through, giving way to sprouts of ugly weeds and moss. The odor was moldy, like the dark corner of a wet basement.

"Probably used for storage," Henry said. "Tools, bags of seed, stuff like that."

They moved closer to the farm, staying close to the trees and tall shrubs. Soon the beekeeping area came into view. The first thing about it the Aldens noticed was that there were fewer hives than on the Shermans' farm.

"No wonder Mr. Hennessey never gets Mr. Price's contract," Jessie said. "He doesn't have half as many bees as the Shermans."

"I'll bet he's not too happy about that," Benny commented.

"No," Henry agreed, "I'll bet he's not. That could be a motive. After all these years of losing the contract just because the Shermans have more bees, what better way to even things out than to make it so the Shermans' bees don't make as much honey as they usually do?"

Violet was studying the whole farm. "Hey, I don't see a field of wildflowers anywhere."

"There must be some flowers around here somewhere," Benny said. "Or else the bees wouldn't be able to survive, would they?"

"No, they wouldn't," Henry said. "But obviously that's another way the Shermans have an edge. It's hard for bees to produce honey when there isn't much nectar to gather."

"But they do have plenty of crops," Violet pointed out, which was true. Hennessey had many more crop fields than the Shermans. Plus, far in the distance, the Aldens saw what appeared to be a few rows of apple trees.

"You know something?" Henry said,

stroking his chin thoughtfully. "I think I'm starting to understand what the Shermans were saying about once having been in business with Hennessey. It all fits together perfectly if you think about it. The Shermans have what Hennessey doesn't, and Hennessey has what the Shermans don't. Together, they've got it all."

"I wonder why they split up," Benny said.

Jessie shook her head. "Who knows? Doesn't seem like something the Shermans are too eager to talk about."

"Maybe we should — "

"Look!" Violet said, pointing.

On the road leading from the house, four men appeared — two in front and two behind them. One of the men in front was wearing a suit and tie. He had a briefcase in one hand and a glass in the other, probably iced tea or lemonade.

The man walking alongside him was old and thin and, judging by the way he moved his hands all around, very irritated about something. Like Clay and Georgie Cooper, he wore a pair of overalls.

"I'll bet that's Mr. Hennessey," Henry said. "He looks like he's in charge, and he's about the right age."

As the four men came closer, the two in the back came into view. One of them was a tall blond-haired boy who looked to be in his mid to late teens. And the other . . .

"Oh, wow!" Benny said excitedly. "That's . . ."

Henry nodded. "That's the guy we chased yesterday."

"Right," Jessie said.

"So he *was* sent to the Shermans' farm by Mr. Hennessey," Violet guessed.

"It appears so," Henry replied.

"I wonder who the man with the brief-case is," Benny said.

"I have no idea," Jessie answered. But that wasn't strictly true — she *did* have an idea, but didn't want to say anything just yet.

The four men stopped at the beekeeping area. "Let's try to get a little closer so we can hear them," Jessie suggested.

"All right, but stay low and keep quiet," Henry advised.

They kept moving until they could hear the voices. The older man and the one in the suit were doing all the talking.

"I really do appreciate you inviting me down to your farm, Mr. Hennessey," the man in the suit said, "and you do have a nice bee colony here. But as I've told you, I still get all the honey I need from the Shermans."

"I know that, Mr. Price, but you may change your mind after you see what I have to show you."

The Aldens looked at one another in astonishment. "It's him!" Violet said in a whisper. "It's Mr. Price! He's visiting earlier than we thought!"

Jessie nodded gravely. "Just as I figured."

"So Mr. Hennessey really is trying to steal the Shermans' business away!"

"Yeah, that's how it sounds."

"What a terrible thing to do," Henry said. "I'll bet that spy he sent over yesterday did put some more Menadrin somewhere. We just didn't see it!"

"I'll bet you're right," Jessie said. Then she smiled. At last, she thought, their first real break.

But then something happened that not only put a quick end to this idea, but also gave the Aldens the biggest shock of the day.

"Take a look at this," Hennessey said to Price. He carefully removed a tray from one of the beehives, turned it upside down, and poured out the exact same whitish fluid that had been flooding the Shermans' hives.

Jessie's mouth fell open. "I . . . I can't believe it. . . ."

"This is what your Mr. Sherman has done to my bees! They aren't producing honey, they're producing *nothing*! It's been like this all year, and it's going to ruin me!"

"How can you be sure it was him?" Mr. Price asked.

"Who else could it be? The Shermans are the only people around here who keep bees for honey! They know I've wanted your contract for years. They also know I was planning on getting more hives after this season. That would make me a real threat!"

Price looked at the milky puddle on the ground. "Well, I have to see the Shermans tomorrow, and I'll keep my eyes and ears open, but . . ."

"But what? Are you actually going to let them get away with this? At least with me you'd be dealing with an honest man!"

Price nodded. "Okay, I'll see what I can find out."

Hennessey seemed happier upon hearing this. He nodded and smiled. "Good. Nice to know someone cares about doing the right thing!"

Henry turned to the others. "I think we'd better get out of here. This is pretty big stuff."

"I'll say," Jessie agreed. "The Shermans will never believe it!"

They started back, making sure they stayed out of view.

As they passed the old farm machinery, however, Benny hooked his foot under a tree root and fell to the soft forest floor —

whump! It sounded like someone punching a pillow.

The four men turned at the same time.

"What was that?" one of them asked.

"I don't know," Hennessey said. "Go over and have a look, quick!"

"Are you okay, Benny?" Jessie whispered.

The youngest Alden got to his knees and brushed himself off. "Yeah, I'm fine. Just dirty."

"Now what?" Violet asked. "They'll see us if we keep going!"

Henry looked around frantically, saw the shed, and got an idea.

"Quick, in there!"

"But they'll look in there!" Jessie said.

"No, I've got something in mind. C'mon, it's our only chance!"

The Aldens scampered into the smelly old shed and crouched down. Only Henry remained standing, peering through the dirty glass of one of the broken windows.

For a moment all was quiet, and Henry thought perhaps the men Hennessey had sent to look had given up.

Then they both came into view, walking slowly, their eyes going over everything.

"Are they there?" Jessie asked softly.

"They sure are," Henry told her, "and they don't look as though they're going to leave in a hurry."

"What are we going to do?" Violet squeaked.

Henry reached into his pocket and brought out a large, flat stone.

"When did you pick that up?" Jessie asked.

"Just now. When I say the word, everyone go back as quietly as you can and hurry to the road. We won't have much time."

The blond-haired kid broke off and moved out of sight. But the other one — the one with the mustache whom they'd chased yesterday — was heading in their direction. He'd be there in less than a minute, and in Henry's mind that minute seemed to be passing faster than any other minute he'd ever known in his life. But he couldn't hurry — this had to be timed just right.

The man looked directly at the shed,

and Henry briefly thought the chance he was hoping for would never come. But then the man turned in the opposite direction. Henry squeezed the rock tight, then tossed it out the window. It landed just where he'd aimed — deep in the bushes where they'd been hiding before.

The man with the mustache scrambled over in that direction with catlike quickness. As soon as he was far enough away, Henry whispered, "Now! Go!"

The Aldens filed out of the shed, smallest to tallest, crouching down like soldiers. Jessie told the others not to look back, just to keep going. But when they got to the road, Henry couldn't resist taking a quick peek. Just as he reached the top, he saw the mustachioed man looking into the shed. Henry knew they were all safe now, but his heart was still pounding.

"All right, let's get out of here," he said breathlessly.

"Fine with me," Benny told him, and the four of them took off running.

CHAPTER 8

Listening In

When the Aldens walked back through the Shermans' door, Clay could tell from their faces that they had discovered something important. His eyes lit up. "The mystery's solved, isn't it?" he asked excitedly.

The children exchanged worried glances. Jessie took a deep breath. "No . . . no, it's not."

Henry nodded. "We saw Mr. Hennessey pouring out trays of watery honey from *his* hive, too. Looks like he's been having the same problems you're having."

"Are you sure?" Dottie asked.

"We all saw it," said Violet sadly.

Clay Sherman's shoulders sagged, and the spirit seemed to drain out of him. "I can't believe it," he said. "I was so sure that Hennessey was behind this, but now . . ."

"Now we're no closer to solving the mystery than we were days ago," said Jessie.

"And Mr. Price is coming by tomorrow," Dottie sighed.

"We're sorry," said Henry.

"You did your best," said Clay. "But I'm sorry, too. And . . . I never thought I'd say this, but I feel kind of bad that old Hennessey has got the same troubles." Dottie nodded at this.

When the Aldens left, the Shermans were discussing how they would make up for the lost money this year. They sounded as though the fight were already over.

The next morning Grandfather took the children to a diner in town to have breakfast. He also wanted to find out everything that had been happening.

"I feel so bad for them," Violet said. "They're such nice people and they're going to lose all that business."

Grandfather nodded sadly as he poured syrup onto his pancakes. "Yes. Unless a miracle happens between now and this afternoon, it looks that way."

"I have to admit," Jessie began, "I've been a little frustrated, too. I mean, I know it sounds selfish, but we haven't been able to get anywhere with this mystery, and that really bothers me."

Her grandfather waved his finger. "No, don't feel like you're being selfish. You kids have put a lot of work into this, and in the past you've always gotten all the pieces of the puzzle together. Anyone would feel frustrated. It just means you care, that's all."

"We haven't gotten any breaks," Henry said. "You need at least a little bit of luck to solve any mystery, and we really haven't had any. At first we thought it was Georgie Cooper, but that turned out to be wrong. Then we thought it was Hennessey, but that turned out to be wrong—"

"You found out about the Menadrin," Grandfather pointed out.

"Yeah, but we need to know who put it there. *That's* the important thing."

Grandfather said, "Maybe there's some way to reverse the Menadrin's effects. At this point I'll bet the Shermans, not to mention Hennessey, would be happy just to get their bees producing honey again. They could always find out who put the Menadrin there later on."

"Have you talked to that nice girl from the lab?" Benny asked. "Renee?"

"No, but I've invited her to the house for dinner tonight. Maybe she'll have some news for us then."

Jessie sighed. "I certainly hope so. We're just about out of time."

Sitting in the corner of the booth, Benny played with his food but didn't eat much — which was unusual, considering his lion-sized appetite. He felt just the way Jessie did — frustrated that they weren't getting anywhere. Could whoever used the Menadrin really be so clever that he or she didn't leave a single clue behind? Is it possible Benny and the others would *never* be able to get to the bottom of this? There was a first time for everything, he supposed, but he didn't want now to be that time.

Then, from the corner of his eye, he noticed a familiar face. A small, roundish man walked into the diner with his suit jacket hung over his arm. He was talking to one of the waitresses and smiling. The waitress was smiling back and laughing, obviously charmed by this new customer. She directed him to a booth not far from the Aldens, and he slid in facing away from them.

Henry was saying something to Grandfather when Benny leaned forward, suddenly feeling very excited, and said in a whisper, "Hey, isn't that the man you and Jessie were talking to on the farm the other day?"

Everyone turned. For a moment they couldn't see his face. But then the waitress came over with a glass of water, and the man turned to thank her.

"Yeah, that's Mr. Carlson," Jessie said. Then, to Grandfather, she added, "He came

to the farm looking for honey, just like you. He was pretty disappointed, but he seemed nice enough."

"Nice enough, except . . ." Henry was still looking at him, his face twisted into a puzzled expression.

"Except what, Henry?" Grandfather asked.

The boy turned back. "Except that he said he was just passing through on his way to visit family. He said he came through every six months or so and stopped by only to get some of the Shermans' honey."

"I wonder why he's still here, then," Violet said.

"Exactly," Henry agreed.

"Maybe his car broke down and he was forced to stay here in town for a few days," Grandfather suggested.

Henry shrugged. "Maybe. I just think it's odd."

Grandfather reached across the table and patted his oldest grandchild on the shoulder. "You're a detective. You're supposed to think certain things seem — "

"Hey, look at that!" Benny cut in again.

Another familiar figure walked into the diner. The Aldens watched in speechless astonishment as the same waitress seated him in the same booth. He reached across the table and shook Mr. Carlson's hand.

"Oh, my goodness," Violet said, "that's . . . that's — "

"It sure is," Jessie cut in, nodding. "It's Mr. Price."

Even Grandfather seemed shocked. "Really? Are you sure?"

"Positive," Henry said. "That's him."

"Well, I suggest you all stop staring and turn back," Grandfather said, "or else he might become suspicious."

"He didn't see us yesterday," Violet told him. "He wouldn't recognize us."

"Still — how would you feel if you looked across a diner and saw four kids staring at you?"

The Aldens turned back and pretended to resume their meal. "Good point," Henry said.

"Boy, I'd love to hear what they're saying," Jessie said. "It would be too risky to go over there, though."

"Especially for you two," Benny said to her and Henry. "If Mr. Carlson turned around, he'd recognize you."

Henry sighed. "With the way our luck's going, I'll bet they're saying some really important stuff, too. Stuff that could help us get to the bottom of things."

Violet shook her head. "If only there was some way . . ."

"I know what you mean," said Henry, staring down at his plate. Suddenly, though, he looked back up. "I've got an idea!" He whispered something to Grandfather, who thought for a moment, then nodded yes.

"What is it?" asked Benny. "Can I help?"

"You sure can," said Henry. "You can eat my bagel!"

Jessie laughed. "What? Why?"

"Because I'm going to order another one!" said Henry, standing up suddenly. He walked across the restaurant to where the two men were sitting and quietly slid into the empty booth just behind them. One of the waitresses, thinking Henry was a new customer, came over to take his order. Then, while he waited for his food, the other Aldens could see him leaning back in his seat slightly in order to hear what Mr. Price and Mr. Carlson were saying.

"Oh, I get it," said Violet, giggling.

"And I'll make sure this bagel gets eaten!" said Benny.

The waitress eventually brought Henry's order — a bagel with butter and a glass of grapefruit juice — and he ate it as if he were any other customer on any other day. About fifteen minutes later, Mr. Price got up, shook hands with Mr. Carlson, and left. Shortly thereafter Mr. Carlson also left, but not before leaving some money on the table to cover the check.

When Henry finally returned to the Aldens' table, the five of them looked at one another with silent smiles. Then the children broke into laughter. The customers seated nearby looked over to see what was so amusing.

Catching her breath, Jessie said, "Okay, so did you hear anything important?"

Still smiling, Henry nodded. "I sure did. I'm glad I went over there."

"Well, tell us," Jessie said. "Don't keep us in the dark!"

"Okay," Henry said. "But I'm not sure you're going to believe this. . . ."

Renee Trowbridge arrived at the Aldens' house for dinner shortly before six o'clock that evening, and she wore the smile of someone who had good news to share. In the Aldens' dining room, Grandfather sat at the head of the long table, the children on either side, and their guest at the other end. Mrs. McGregor, their housekeeper, had made roast chicken with red potatoes and vegetables, including some string beans Grandfather had bought at the Shermans' farm. It smelled irresistible.

"So I think you'd better tell us your big news," Grandfather said to Renee as they began passing bowls around. "I doubt the

kids can cover up their curiosity with po-
liteness much longer."

"And we have some news, too!" Benny
said, beaming with excitement. Jessie
handed him a basket of hot rolls, and he
took two without even looking. "Some really big news!"

Renee smiled. "That's great. Well, I guess
I'll go first. It turns out," she began, "there
is a way to stop the effects of Menadrin."

Violet responded first. "You're kidding!"

"Nope. What happens is it just wears off.
That is, of course, unless you keep spraying
it on the flowers."

"That's great, Renee," Grandfather said.

"Except it probably takes a while, right,
Renee?" asked Henry.

"You guessed it. Three weeks, at least,"
Renee answered.

Grandfather shrugged. "Well, it's better
than nothing. At least the Shermans and
Hennessey can get their bees going again.
What else, Renee?"

Renee reached down into her briefcase by
her chair and pulled out a folder filled with

news clippings. "I did a little research and found out that Menadrin was produced by a chemical company called Pioneer Laboratories. They were based in New Jersey, which, as you know, is not too far from here. They thought they'd invented a miracle potion for growing fruits and vegetables, like I said a few days ago, and they were so sure it was going to be a hit that they produced tons and tons of it. They poured a lot of money into the project. It was a huge risk, but they gambled that there would be no side effects." She raised one eyebrow and said, "They were wrong."

"Sounds like someone lost a load of money," Grandfather observed.

Renee nodded. "Sure did. Someone lost a *fortune*."

"Wow!" Jessie said.

Benny couldn't keep quiet about their own news any longer. "We were in the diner this morning, and we saw Mr. Price talking to another man, a man we saw on the Shermans' farm a few days ago. When we first saw him, he told us his name was

Mr. Carlson, but when Henry overheard them talking, Mr. Price called him Mr. Wentworth."

"*Tyler* Wentworth," Henry added.

"Oh, my goodness," said Renee. "He was the owner of Pioneer Laboratories!"

She pulled a magazine article out of her folder and showed it to the Aldens. One of the pages showed a man's photograph with the caption *Tyler Wentworth*, and the children recognized him instantly.

"Let me guess — he's the man who lost all the money, right?" said Henry.

Renee nodded. "That's right. He lost so much that he had to go out of business. No one's heard much about him since. It probably ruined him."

Grandfather said, "This is starting to make sense now. I'll bet the first thing that was on Tyler Wentworth's mind when he learned that he was going to lose all that money was how to get it back."

"By making it so the Shermans' bees didn't produce any more honey?" Renee asked. "That doesn't make sense."

"Unless Mr. Wentworth decided to go into the honey business himself," said Henry. "And from what I overheard today, he has!"

"You mean the reason Wentworth was talking to Mr. Price was because he was trying to get that big contract?" asked Renee.

"And it was very good for him that both Sherman and Hennessey were having trouble with their bees at the same time," Violet added. "That meant Mr. Price would be stuck, right, Grandfather? And he'd have to buy honey from someone else."

"That's right," Grandfather said.

"In fact," said Henry, "that's exactly what they were talking about in the diner — the contract. Still, I suppose it could be a coincidence. I wish we had one more clue."

"Wait," said Jessie. "I remember Mr. Wentworth had all these red marks on his arms. Could that be a sign that he was the one who sprayed the Menadrin on the wildflowers?"

"It certainly could be," Renee told her. "Menadrin is known to cause mild rashes on the skin, even without direct contact. If you sprayed it without gloves and long sleeves and the wind blew it back onto you . . . sure, you could very easily develop a rash."

Everyone fell silent as they considered what this meant.

Violet said, "I think this is the big break we've needed."

"So what's next?" Renee asked.

"I think it's time to give the Shermans a call," Henry said.

CHAPTER 9

A Fair Price

Everyone ate quickly, then piled into the station wagon and headed over to the Shermans' farm. At one point in the journey Grandfather joked that they were "making a *beeline*" over there, but instead of laughter all he got was a round of groans.

The Shermans were pretty depressed when the Aldens arrived.

"John Price came by today," sighed Dottie, "and it was so hard to tell him that we don't have any honey."

Clay was slumped in his chair. "He said he had no choice but to find someone else this year. Can't say I blame him."

"Oh, no," gasped Violet. She hated to see them so upset. *Maybe we're too late to help them*, she thought.

"Mr. Price is a good man, though," Dottie was saying. "He said he'll check back with us next season to see if we've got honey."

"He even said he'd give the contract back to us *this* season if we could somehow come up with enough honey in these next two months before the delivery date," said Clay, though clearly he didn't think this was possible.

"Well, Mr. Sherman, you just might be able to pull it off," said Renee. Soon she and the Aldens were telling the Shermans all their news. "Trust me, the Menadrin will wear off in time," she told Clay and Dottie.

"Thank goodness!" said Dottie. But Clay still had a reason to be upset.

"You mean this Tyler Wentworth fellow

is trying to ruin my honey business?" he asked.

"Unfortunately, that seems to be the case," said Grandfather. "Only we need some proof."

Henry, who had been thinking quietly, spoke up. "I think I've got a plan."

"You do?" asked Jessie. "And what would that be?"

Henry smiled, then told them.

The Aldens, the Shermans, and Renee drove to the little hotel in town where John Price was staying for the night.

Mr. Price was wearing dark pants and a white shirt when he opened the door, but he'd taken off his jacket, tie, and shoes. The TV was on, and a newspaper lay open on the bed. Mr. Price looked as though he hadn't been expecting any visitors but got a whole load of them instead.

"Can I, uh . . . help you?" he asked.

The Shermans stepped forward. "Hello again, John," Mr. Sherman said.

Mr. Price wanted to smile, but he was still too puzzled. "Hi, Clay. What's this all about?"

"Can we come in for a few minutes?" Mr. Sherman asked.

"Sure, if there's room. Maybe I should move the bed into the parking lot," Mr. Price joked.

"I don't think that'll be necessary," said Mr. Sherman with a weak smile.

Once everyone was settled — the adults in chairs and the Alden children sitting cross-legged on the big bed — and all the introductions had been made, Mr. Price said, "So, what's going on?"

"You've been in contact with a man named Wentworth, is that correct?" Henry asked.

"Well, yes, in fact I have." Mr. Price nodded toward the Shermans. "He'll be taking over the Shermans' honey contract, unless they can come up with enough before the delivery date."

"Mr. Wentworth isn't who he seems," Jessie said.

Mr. Price's eyebrows rose. "What do you mean? He assured me he could supply the honey I needed. Had pictures of his hives and everything. Even invited me to come look at them next week."

"In New Jersey, right?" Henry asked.

John Price looked a little stunned. "Well . . . yes. How'd you know that?"

Henry told Mr. Price everything that had been happening over the last few days, with Renee adding some scientific details about the Menadrin. As Henry went deeper into the story, Mr. Price looked more and more shocked.

When Henry was finished, Mr. Price said, "I . . . I can't believe this. Would someone really go to all that trouble, just to get this contract?"

"When you've lost as much money as he has," Grandfather Alden said, "you probably get desperate. I'm sure he knows what he's doing is wrong, but he's probably gone beyond the point of caring."

Mr. Price looked at the Shermans. "I'm really sorry about this. I assure you I won't be giving that contract to Tyler Went-worth."

"Well . . . we're not *positive* it's him," Vi-olet said cautiously.

"No, that's why we came over here," Jessie added.

"Who else could it be?" Mr. Price said, holding up his hands. "It all fits so perfectly. But how are you going to get this proof you need?" he asked the children. "If he's the one, he's not just going to say, 'You're right, it was me!' "

"Henry has a plan," Clay Sherman said, "and from the sound of it, it's a darn good one."

Mr. Price turned to the boy. "Is that right? Let's hear it."

So Henry told him everything from be-ginning to end. When he was finished, Mr. Price said, "That sounds like it just might work."

"It should," Henry agreed, "but we'll re-ally need your help. That's key. How about it?"

John Price thought it over for a moment,

then smiled. "Sure. I've never caught a criminal before."

"Then this'll be your big chance," Jessie told him.

The Aldens returned to Mr. Price's hotel early the next morning, along with their grandfather, and went over phase one of Henry's plan.

"Sounds good," said Mr. Price. "Are you ready?" he asked the children.

"Ready," said Benny.

Mr. Price picked up the hotel phone and pressed the speakerphone button so the Aldens could listen in. Then he dialed the number on Tyler Wentworth's business card. Wentworth picked it up on the second ring.

"Hello?"

"Mr. Wentworth? John Price here. We spoke over breakfast yesterday morning."

"John! How are you doing this morning, my friend?"

"I'm fine, Tyler, just fine. Hey, listen, I've got some bad news for you, I'm afraid." Mr. Price looked at the Aldens and winked.

"Bad news? What might that be?"

"Well, I don't know how, but the bees on the Shermans' farm have started making honey again. Remember when I called before and said you could have the contract because their bees had stopped? Well, I just got off the phone with Mrs. Sherman, and she said everything was going fine again."

Mr. Price waited for Tyler Wentworth to say something, but there was only silence.

"Tyler? You still there?"

"Huh? Oh, um . . . yeah, sure, I'm still here." He gave a small laugh, but there wasn't any humor in it. "Well, that's great, John. Just great. I'm glad to hear it, I'm glad for them. What was happening over there was just terrible. Good for them, really."

"I just wanted you to know right away," Mr. Price went on. "No hard feelings, I hope? They've been my honey people for a long time, and I believe in loyalty. It's only fair."

"Huh? Oh, no, no hard feelings at all," Wentworth told him, and he almost sounded like he meant it. "No hard feelings. Okay, well, maybe next season?"

"Sure, maybe," Mr. Price said. "For now, I wish you the best of luck selling your honey elsewhere."

"What? Oh, sure, yes, thanks. Thanks very much."

There was another pause, and then Wentworth said, "Hey, listen, if their bees go through that strange spell again, would you still take the honey from me?"

John Price smiled broadly and gave the Aldens a thumbs-up.

"I sure would," Mr. Price said enthusiastically. "I'd have to. I'd have no one else to turn to!"

A much happier Tyler Wentworth said, "Great, then please keep me in mind."

"I sure will," Mr. Price said. "Have a good day."

After he hung up the phone, he put his hand up and each Alden gave him a high five.

"Like a fish taking a worm," he said cheerfully.

"You were perfect," Jessie said. "Perfect."

"Yeah, you almost had me fooled," Benny said.

"Maybe I should give up the food business and go into acting," Mr. Price said, admiring himself in the mirror.

Henry said, "Okay, everyone ready for phase two?"

"Wouldn't miss it for the world," Mr. Price replied.

"Good. Let's go."

CHAPTER 10

The Poisoner's Return

The Aldens hid among the wildflowers close to the Menadrin-infected spot Violet had discovered days before. Grandfather, Mr. Price, and the Shermans stayed in the house, where they watched with a pair of binoculars through a second-floor window.

Two hours passed, and when the sun started rising above the trees, the temperature rose with it.

"It's starting to get hot," Benny said, sitting cross-legged with his brother and sisters.

"And the smell," Jessie said, pinching her nose and making a face. "I like wildflowers as much as anybody, but this is too much!"

Henry nodded. "I know it's hard, but we've got to follow the plan. If my guess is right, there should be — "

A crunching sound. It came from somewhere in the woods.

"Did you hear that?" Henry asked in a whisper.

"I sure did!" Benny said.

"Okay, if Grandfather and the others are watching, which I'm sure they are, then they're already taking care of their part of the plan. Now let's take care of ours."

Crouching down, the Aldens moved slowly through the wildflowers, splitting up to cover as wide an area as possible.

Henry believed Wentworth would return with more Menadrin and use it in the same spot he did last time. He reached the edge of the field and cautiously peeked out to have a look. Sure enough, his guess was right.

Tyler Wentworth was standing there with a small pump-spray bottle in hand.

Following the plan, Henry stepped out and said firmly, "I wouldn't do that if I were you, Mr. Wentworth. You're in enough trouble already."

Wentworth jumped, totally caught off guard, and the bottle tumbled to the ground. The other three Aldens stepped from the wildflowers and surrounded him.

"What . . . what's the meaning of — "

"We know all about your plan to steal Mr. Price's honey contract away from the Shermans," Jessie said, sounding very angry. "How could you do something like that?"

"Huh? I don't have to stand here and listen to this from a bunch of kids!"

The Aldens closed in around him.

"Yes, you do," Henry said. "We're not the only ones who know. Mr. Price knows, and so do the Shermans and Mr. Hennessey. And believe me, they're not too happy about it."

"If you were smart, you'd give up now," Jessie said. "Before you make things worse."

"Yeah!" Benny added for good measure.

Tyler Wentworth took a step back, then noticed the spray bottle lying nearby.

"Don't let him get that!" Jessie yelled, and Henry went for it.

For a man so small and pudgy, Tyler Wentworth was pretty fast. But Henry was a little bit faster, and he got it. He nearly bumped Wentworth's head with his own as he snatched the bottle from the ground.

Jumping back, Henry said, "Nice try, but I don't think so."

Flustered and angry, Wentworth came forward with his hand out. "Gimme that!" he barked.

Henry tossed the bottle to Violet. "Catch!" he said.

Wentworth turned to her. "Come on now!"

When he went forward, Violet pitched it to Benny. "Here, Benny!"

Wentworth now turned to him. "Son," he said, "c'mon, give it up." As he stepped forward, Benny threw it to Jessie.

The Aldens continued to distract Mr. Wentworth by tossing the bottle to one another until the adults arrived — along with two members of Greenfield's police department. When Wentworth saw the police, he tried to escape into the woods — but Jack Hennessey was there with his two men to head him off.

"Just hold on there a moment, my friend," Hennessey said sharply. "You're not going anywhere."

Tyler Wentworth looked in all directions, hoping to find an escape route. But there wasn't one. His luck had finally run out. His head dropped and his shoulders sagged.

"How could you do such a thing?" Grandfather Alden asked him. "What were you thinking?"

"I was thinking about the money I lost," Wentworth said quietly. "How the Menadrin almost ruined me. You don't know what it's like to lose that much money."

"So you thought you'd ruin someone else's business to make up for it? That was your idea for fixing the problem?" Henry asked. Tyler Wentworth didn't have any reply to that. He just stared at the ground and said nothing.

"You're going to have a lot of explaining to do to a lot of people," Grandfather told him. "This little plan of yours will probably finish off whatever chances you had of getting back on your feet."

Wentworth nodded. "It was a risk. I knew that all along."

"A risk that didn't pay off," Jessie reminded him.

"No, I guess it didn't."

The Greenfield police came and took him away. Five minutes later he was sitting in the back of their squad car, on his way to the station.

Clay Sherman and Jack Hennessey were asked to follow the police down to the station to give their side of the story. While they were there, the Aldens went back home to rest.

Soon after the Aldens arrived home, Clay

and Dottie called to ask if they would come back to the farm later that evening.

"We've got a special surprise for you and your grandchildren," Dottie told James Alden over the phone.

Grandfather smiled. "Okay, Dottie, we'll be there."

He hung up the phone thinking he and the children would soon be receiving some honey, free of charge. The Shermans were wonderful people, Grandfather thought as he headed toward the living room to tell the kids about the invitation, but, he decided firmly, he wasn't going to take any more than one jar of honey for each of them. The Shermans had a lot of catching up to do with their honey business this season, so the last thing they needed was to be giving it all away. The children were thrilled at the idea of going back to the farm, and they agreed with their grandfather that one jar apiece would be more than enough.

They arrived shortly after five o'clock, parked in the driveway by the backyard, and knocked on the door.

"What's that wonderful smell?" Violet wondered aloud, sniffing the warm evening air.

Henry nodded. "Yeah, something smells great."

Benny was just about to add his two cents when Mr. Sherman opened the door. "Welcome back. We're glad you could make it," he said.

"It's nice of you to invite us," Henry replied. "Thank you."

"Do you have a fire going?" Jessie asked.

Clay smiled. "Well, not exactly. Come on," he told them. "You'll see."

They went back into the house, down the hallway, and into a room they hadn't seen before. Clay's smile grew wider.

As soon as they entered the dining room, Clay turned around and said, "Surprise!"

The Aldens were delighted by what they saw. Jessie spoke for all of them. "Oh, my goodness! This is . . . just lovely!"

The Aldens weren't sure they had ever seen a dinner quite so wonderful as the one laid out on the Shermans' table.

First there was the turkey itself, in the center on a silver platter, cooked to a perfect golden brown. Steam rose from it in gentle wisps, and it actually shone in the light of the chandelier.

Surrounding the turkey were bowls of side dishes: cranberry sauce, mashed potatoes, baked potatoes, corn on the cob, peas, string beans, honey-glazed carrots, mint jelly, and baskets of soft biscuits.

What made the meal even more impressive was the careful way it had been laid out. The Shermans had covered the table in a lace tablecloth, and they'd gotten out their best silver.

"Clay . . . Dottie . . . this is just lovely," Grandfather said. "You didn't have to go to all this tr — "

"Nonsense," Dottie said, still wearing her apron. "You all deserve this, and more, for helping us save our honey business."

"It's beautiful," Violet told her. "Just . . . perfect."

The others nodded as if Violet had found the best word.

"Well, I had a little help from Dottie, of course," Clay said jokingly.

Dottie swatted him lightly with a hand towel. "Married over thirty years and he still thinks he's a comedian."

"What are we waiting for?" Clay asked. "Let's eat!"

They all sat, tucked their napkins into their shirts, and dug in.

"Can you tell us what happened down at the police station?" Henry asked Mr. Sherman as he cut through a slice of meat. "If no one minds talking about this over dinner."

Clay said, "Well, from the moment Jack Hennessey and I got there until we left, Tyler Wentworth insisted that what he'd done wasn't all that wrong, and that any of us would've done the same thing in his position. He kept talking about all that money he'd lost."

Jessie shook her head. "He has a strange sense of what's right and what's wrong."

"All he sees is the money," Grandfather said. "Nothing else matters to someone like that."

"Was anything said about what would happen to him?" Henry asked.

"Well," Clay said, "it's certain he's going to be paying a lot of fines."

"Do you think he's out of the chemical business?" Benny asked.

"That's for sure," Clay said. "His license to make chemicals will be taken away as soon as the government hears about this."

"What a shame," Grandfather said. "A man with so much knowledge and business skill turning bad like that."

"I'll bet if he would've worked harder on something else, he could have made up for all the money he lost," Violet suggested.

"You're probably right," Clay replied. "But instead he chose to do something evil, and now he's lost everything."

Everyone was quiet for a moment, thinking about Mr. Wentworth's troubles.

Jessie spoke next. "You might say he's got one *honey* of a problem on his hands."

The children started laughing first.

"Yeah," added Henry, "he sure got himself into a sticky situation!"

Now the adults joined in and the dining room rang with laughter.

"It certainly feels nice to have a good laugh," Mr. Sherman said, "after the worry of the last several days." Then he said, "Speaking of honey, that reminds me . . ." and got up from the table. He disappeared into the kitchen for a few minutes, then returned with five small, colorfully wrapped boxes with bows on top.

"This is another little thank-you for each of you. The first of a new batch."

He handed out the boxes to the Aldens, who began unwrapping them. Inside the boxes were jars of homemade honey from the Shermans' farm.

But when they took the jars out, they noticed something different on the labels — where it used to say, MADE AT SHERMAN FARM, GREENFIELD, CONNECTICUT, it now said, MADE AT NORTH STAR FARMS, GREEN-FIELD, CONNECTICUT.

"Isn't this supposed to say 'Sherman Farm' at the bottom?" Benny asked.

"Why the change in name?" Grandfather asked.

Clay smiled at Dottie, and she smiled back.

"No, the name is right. It's an old name, actually," he said. "The original name of this farm, back when we were first making honey."

"The original name?" Jessie asked. "Why'd you change back?"

"How about letting our new partners explain the name change?" Clay said to Dottie.

The Alden children looked at Clay in mild confusion.

At that moment, Jack Hennessey and his wife, Lorraine, walked into the room, smiling happily.

"Hi, everybody!" Jack said cheerfully. "Mind if we join you?"

Conveniently there were two empty places at the table. The Aldens had noticed them before, but hadn't wanted to ask about them.

Jessie said, "You mean . . ."

"That's right," Clay replied, coming behind Jack and putting his hands on Jack's shoulders. "From now on, we're back in business together. All four of us."

"That's wonderful!" Violet said.

"All these years we've been mad at each other," Jack said, "and it's been so long that neither of us remembers what we were so angry about."

Clay smiled. "You know how stubborn people can be sometimes."

Dottie rolled her eyes. "Do we ever."

Lorraine Hennessey reached over and put her hand on Dottie's. "At least we can be friends again without having to keep it a secret."

Clay and Jack both looked puzzled. "What?" they both asked.

"Oh, Jack," Lorraine said, "you don't think Dottie and I were going to stop being friends just because you two did, do you?"

Jack pointed, moving his finger between the two ladies. "You mean you've been . . . ?"

Dottie smiled slyly. "That's right. We wanted no part of your ridiculous fight."

The Aldens all smiled. Clay and Jack looked at each other in astonishment.

"How do you like that?" Clay said. "Here we went to all the trouble to be mad at each other all these years, and the whole time our wives were best friends."

Jack shook his head. "Just goes to show how much smarter they are than us, I guess."

Now everyone laughed.

Grandfather stood and held his glass in the air. "I'd like to propose a toast," he said. "To North Star Farms. May they never have anything but the greatest success."

Everyone cheered.

Then Clay Sherman rose and lifted his own glass. "And here's to the Aldens. May they solve their next mystery just as neatly as they solved this one."

Henry, Jessie, Violet, and Benny agreed enthusiastically. And each wondered what new challenges that next mystery would bring.

GERTRUDE CHANDLER WARNER discovered when she was teaching that many readers who like an exciting story could find no books that were both easy and fun to read. She decided to try to meet this need, and her first book, *The Boxcar Children*, quickly proved she had succeeded.

Miss Warner drew on her own experiences to write the mystery. As a child she spent hours watching trains go by on the tracks opposite her family home. She often dreamed about what it would be like to set up housekeeping in a caboose or freight car — the situation the Alden children find themselves in.

When Miss Warner received requests for more adventures involving Henry, Jessie, Violet, and Benny Alden, she began additional stories. In each, she chose a special setting and introduced unusual or eccentric characters who liked the unpredictable.

While the mystery element is central to each of Miss Warner's books, she never thought of them as strictly juvenile mysteries. She liked to stress the Aldens' independence and resourcefulness and their solid New England devotion to using up and making do. The Aldens go about most of their adventures with as little adult supervision as possible — something else that delights young readers.

Miss Warner lived in Putnam, Connecticut, until her death in 1979. During her lifetime, she received hundreds of letters from girls and boys telling her how much they liked her books.

A Sticky Situation!

Grandfather Alden has a sweet tooth for the best honey in the world — Sherman Farm honey. But when he and the children get to the farm, they discover that the bees have stopped making honey and there is no honey for sale this year. It's a real mystery, but Henry, Jessie, Violet, and Benny will find a way to solve this sticky situation.

Now you can *bee* detectives and find some puzzling mysteries, too. Just grab your pencils and get started on the puzzles and games on the next few pages. You can check your answers at the back of the book. Good luck, and get buzzing. . . .

Bee Hunt

The Boxcar Children learned lots of new words that have to do with making honey while they were at the Shermans' farm. Can you help them find the words in the search below? The words go up, down, sideways, backward, and diagonally. Look for: CELLS, COMB, DRONES, EGGS, HIVE, HONEY, NECTAR, QUEEN, WAX, WILD-FLOWERS, WORKERS

```
X  I  W  R  W  A  W
H  D  I  A  I  I  X
I  S  L  T  X  L  D
V  L  D  C  C  Y  R
E  L  F  E  E  U  Q
G  E  L  N  M  S  U
G  C  O  M  B  E  E
S  H  W  O  Q  N  E
Q  U  E  E  N  O  X
W  O  R  K  E  R  S
E  N  S  O  R  D  S
```

A Scrambled Breakfast

The Aldens — especially Benny — loved the country breakfast Mrs. Sherman served at the farm. Unscramble the words below to find out what they ate.

1. caobn _____

2. kaapcens _____

3. pyurs _____

4. defri gseg _____

5. uibtsics _____

6. egoanr ciuje _____

It's Good to BEE Different!

The Aldens found out that something strange was going on at the Shermans' farm. And there's something strange about one of the bee towers below. Look closely at the bee towers and circle the one that is different from the rest.

A Sweet Memory

When you're a detective like the Aldens, you have to be very observant and have a good memory. Now it's your turn to act like a detective. Study the farm scene below. Try to remember everything you can. Then turn the page. . . .

Now look carefully at this picture. On the lines to the right, write down all the things that are different from the last picture.

Where Can They Bee?

Henry, Jessie, Violet, and Benny spent a lot of time in the field of wildflowers searching for clues. Now you can search for something, too — bees! There are fifteen bees hidden in this picture. Circle the ones you find.

Better BEE Quick!

The Aldens have spotted their suspect. Help them chase him down before he gets away!

START

SUSPECT CAUGHT!

Pesky Pesticides

The Aldens learned a lot about pesticides while trying to solve this mystery. Using the letters in the word *pesticide*, see how many three-, four-, and five-letter words you can make. Here are some clues to get you started:

 **PESTICIDE**

1. A man might wear it around his neck. (3 letters)

_____

2. You can take a small or a giant one. (4 letters)

_____

3. The opposite of shallow. (4 letters)

_____

4. You could get a ticket if you do this. (5 letters)

_____

5. A dog, or a cat, or a fish. (3 letters)

_____

Make a Beeline

Connect the dots to find out what this mystery picture is.

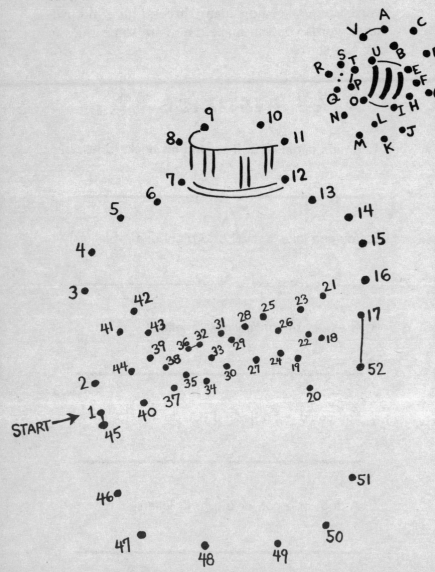

Answers to the Puzzles
Bee Hunt

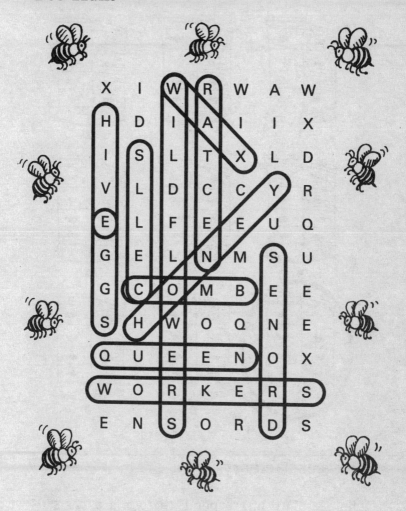

A Scrambled Breakfast

1. bacon
2. pancakes
3. syrup
4. fried eggs
5. biscuits
6. orange juice

It's Good to BEE Different!

A Sweet Memory

The geese are in the pond; there is a paper sail-boat floating in the pond; there are only two chickens; there is a dog; there is no cat; there is a rooster on top of the henhouse; there are no bees; there is a bee tower; there are wildflowers growing near the pond; and there is a hole in the fence.

Where can they BEE?

Better BEE QUICK!

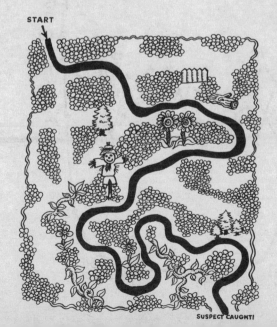

START

SUSPECT CAUGHT!

Pesky Pesticides

1. tie 2. step 3. deep 4. speed 5. pet

other possible answers: cede, cite, dice, die, disc, pest, pie, side, steep, tide

Make a Beeline

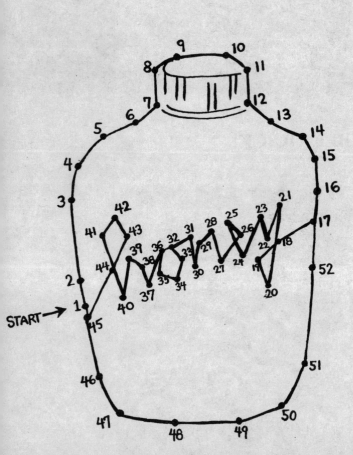